THE EXORCISM
And
OTHER SHORT STORIES

AUTHOR: KHALIL ISAAC MATHAI

EDITING AND COVER DESIGN: JIBIN JAMES

Index

Page left blank Intentionally

The Exorcism

Little Jessica was possessed by an evil spirit. Her parents fondly remembered how charming Jessica had been before the spirit possessed her. She had been the most lovable baby in the nursery of the busy maternity home, where she was born. The young nurses would fight amongst themselves for the privilege of holding her and playing with her. Her mother Veronica, was confined to bed after her caesarian. These foster caretakers were the ones who would change nappies and powder the little baby girl. Jessica was really an angel child. She never bawled for milk. When her nappies were wet, she would look around sheepishly till some one noticed. She was a welcome contrast to the other newborns in the nursery.

After going home too she was everyone's pet. Where other babies demanded attention. Jessica had attention thrust upon her. Normally reticent nephews and nieces were ready and eager to baby sit her. Jessica was content in her play pen, studying the assorted toys she regularly received. When she started going to play school, she was the easiest to manage, in addition to being the sweetest looking.

It was soon after her fifth birthday that things started going horribly wrong. Jessica had just come back from her new school. Veronica had laid out the clothes for Jessica to change into. Minutes later when she came back to investigate- Veronica was shocked to see Jessica, standing where she had left her- in the middle of the room. She had passed urine in her school uniform, and stood there, shivering uncontrollably.

Her mother screamed and ran to her. She tried to hug Jessica- but the girl fought her off her with all her strength. She scratched her mother's face, screaming profanities no five-year-old could here picked up. Veronica was desperately trying to hold her. Jessica seemed to have acquired the strength of an adult. Suddenly the thrashing stopped. Jessica's body went limp. Her eyes rolled up and she frothed at the mouth. Veronica carried her to the bed and laid her down on it. She then dialed for her pediatrician and called her husband John.

The doctor was sympathetic. He listened patiently to Veronica's account. The girl had surely suffered a seizure. She was sleeping serenely now. Only a thin trickle blood from her lip, and the scratches on Veronica's face gave some inkling of the events that had unfolded a while ago. Veronica had trained as a nurse, although she had never worked as one. She had been a witness to other's seizures. She had not seen even anything remotely as horrific as the one her daughter had suffered. The profanities Jessica had yelled while she struggled with her had been so deviant and so adult. It was unbelievable that a child, even during a seizure could not have uttered them.

The doctor was firm. Temporal lobe epilepsy could occur with behavioral aberrations. He was sure Veronica was over reacting. He prescribed a drug which would keep the 'complex partial seizures' in check. He arranged an appointment for Jessica with the consultant neurologist.

The neurologist was very considerate and charming. He concurred with the pediatrician's diagnosis. He would get an MRI Scan of Jessica's brain over the weekend. He also ordered an electroencephalogram. He increased the dosage of anti-seizure drugs the pediatrician had prescribed and added another. With these medicines – he assured the anxious parents- there would be no more seizures. Only partly reassured, they returned to their home. That evening, Jessica had her next attack

Hearing Veronica scream, John rushed into the bed room. Jessica was sitting on the bed, a pair of scissors in her hands. She was cutting up a beautiful gown he had presented to Veronica for their anniversary. Veronica's hands were bleeding profusely. Jessica had lunged at her with the scissors when she had tried to take it from her. Jessica's eyes were blood shot and she was muttering profanities. It took John all his strength to wrestle the scissors from his daughter. He almost lost an eye in the process. Jessica's strength amazed him. This was no seizure. As Jessica drifted off into deep sleep, the parents took stock. They had no option but to take her back to the hospital. But they were increasingly skeptical about the seizure hypothesis.

At the hospital, the neurologist was concerned and sympathetic. Jessica was admitted into the pediatric intensive care unit. Heavily sedated, she slept through the night. The next morning, she underwent an MRI scan. With her history of violent behavior, the scan had to be under anesthesia.

Jessica's MRI Scan was unusual- to say the least. There was a large tumor in the center of her brain- near the hypothalamus. Hamartomas or abnormal aggregations of otherwise normal tissue were not unusual in this part of the brain. Her tumor was almost like a miniature brain in itself.

An unusual hamartoma in the hypothalamic region- the radiologist opined. Jessica's next evaluation was an electroencephalogram. This would read the electrical activity of the different parts of her brain. It would help the neurologist to focus on areas giving unsynchronized discharges or spikes. Jessica's electroencephalogram record was bizarre. There were spike discharges from all over the cerebral cortex. It suggested a deep focus dominating all other areas of Jessica's brain. When they shaved Jessica's head for the EEG they noted a scar on Jessica's scalp. It was a neat scar one inch long. It looked as if a neat cut had been made. Under the scalp too, was a crack in the bone that had now healed. Children with seizures often fell. This was the doctor's conclusion. John and Veronica looked at each other. They could remember no injury. The cut was so neat. Had someone or something messed about with their daughters' brain?

Jessica's medications were changed. Consultations with the best of specialists followed. The decision was unanimous. The tumor in hypothalamic region should come out. There was a possibility that the seizures could still persist. The growth had grafted for itself feeding blood vessels from every important brain artery. Surgical resection would be fraught with problems. But the risk had to be taken.

John and Veronica had an uncle who was a missionary priest. He came to visit Jessica. By now Jessica was back home. A special room had been made for her- where she could not harm herself. Her fits persisted. They would last an hour or two and occurred once or twice a day. John and Veronica took turns to be at her side. The priest sensed something spiritually amiss. The doors of Jessica's room banged shut on their own before he could enter. The electrical fuse blew and the house was plunged to darkness. Jessica had a fit so explosive that it took all Johns strength to hold her back. She tried to charge her uncle and then tried to jump out of her window. The priest backed out slowly clutching a cross in his hand. Slowly Jessica's fury abated, as she sank into her post seizure sleep

The priest called John to his room at the monastery. Jessica was possessed; the missionary was sure of that. John told him of the surgeons' plans to remove the tumor from child's brain. Was this tumor an embodiment of the spirit that possessed her?

The missionary had a consultation with the devout. There was a wing in the monastery where they researched antidotes to black magic. The church had never publicized it for fears of a public outcry. They had many thinkers in their midst, even holy men of other religions. One of the missionaries had been a neurologist. He studied the scans with care. The spirit which possessed her had embodied itself by creating a mini-brain in Jessica's mind. To attempt to exorcise this spirit by prayer alone could be futile. They however knew that the spirit would repulse any attempt by a surgeon to destroy his abode.

The surgical team which planned to tackle Jessica's tumor had been flown in from Europe. The scrub nurse Janet, who was to assist the surgery was taken into confidence by the missionary. A special instrument was crafted. This resembled a bayonet shaped forceps. It was crafted out of silver which had been smelted out of the base of a holy chalice. The sister was entrusted to encourage the neurosurgeon to use the instrument. They could not tell the surgeon more. Like most excellent technicians he could be averse to mixing up science and spirituality.

The day of the surgery dawned. Jessica was wheeled in, away from her tearful parents. In the anesthesia console they sedated her. They then passed another wide bore cannula to access her veins and a tube to ventilate her lungs. An array of gadgets was hooked on. During surgery they would monitor her pulse, blood pressure, temperature and the concentrations of various gases and drugs in her blood. Another monitor checked on her brain waves. Abnormal spiky discharges from all the EEG leads illustrated the underlying irritative focus.

Jessica was then wheeled into the operating suite. Jennet had placed the silver forceps on the surgeons' tray. The cut in the scalp was made with finesse. Bleeding vessels were burned off. The cut in the skull was next. This was done with a pneumatic oscillating saw. A neat circle of bone was removed and handed over to Janet, who placed it in a bowl of sterile saline. The dura-mater, the thick fibrous covering of the brain was cut next. The surgeon – a master of his craft opened out one of the fluid conduits or cisterns. As the brain fluid escaped in to the suction apparatus- the brain relaxed and became softer. In the depth the tumor could be seen now. Red and angry looking- it pulsated dangerously.

Suddenly all hell broke loose. The heart started racing uncontrollably. The blood pressure which had been kept steady by the anesthetic team was having a roller coaster ride. The tumor was swelling before their eyes. The surgeon immediately realized that the things were going out his control. Malignant brain Edema could be impossible to handle. With the limited access he had, there was nothing he could do to the tumor.

This poor girl, whose parents had trusted him, was going to die on the table.

Janet remembered the silver bayonet. She used the forceps to pick up a small cotton piece and place it on the tumor. This was normally the prerogative of the surgeons' assistant. But they were all paralysed- their eyes were on the monitor with the alarms and red flashes gone haywire. Janet placed the cotton piece into the wound and then touched the swelling tumor with her bayonet. The surgeon opened his mouth to chastise her- but stopped. Something miraculous was happening. In front of their eyes, the brain was setting down. The blood pressure stabilized and the heart rate was stable once more. Janet's eyes met the surgeons. There was an unspoken communication, born of years of trust and association.

Unobtrusively the chief surgeon moved his assistant across, so that Janet could keep her place and her forceps undisturbed. The surgeon was back at his job. He coagulated and cut the tortuous blood vessels feeding the tumor, with precision. In an hour, the surgery was over- the tumor- impaled in Janet's forceps was pulled out of Jessica's brain. It was be washed in the sluice room and then placed in a preservative for microscopic study.

Jessica made a remarkable recovery. She was well. She became the same lovable angel girl, her parents and friends had known before. She would be back at school within a month. Her father took her to the surgeon for a review. Everything was perfect. The only irritant was the histopathology of the tumor. The tumor which they had packed and sent for histopathological examination was missing. The pathologists claimed that the bottle had been empty when they received it.

Jessica wore a small cross around her neck always for protection. It was made of silver. Her missionary uncle had gifted it to her. She was safe now.

*****

The Old Man

The old man sat under the tree. This had become a regular feature in his daily agenda for over five years. The only time, he deviated from the routine was when his son Puttu, officially- Lance Naik Putudar Sanu, came home on leave. Today his son would be back. He walked back into his hut. The army was generous with leave for its soldiers. Ten months of the year, they flogged them. Then, for two months they were sent home on leave. A soldier's leave was sacrosanct. Leave was denied only when the nation was at war. During national emergencies soldiers on leave and even reservists would be recalled.

The life of an army man was ironclad in organizational discipline. The soldier's day started well before sunrise. In peace stations, there would be a morning session of physical training. Then there were roads to be laid, ditches to be dug, weapons to be maintained and innumerable other jobs till evening, when it was time for unit games. The old man's son Puttu played football and was in the regimental team. In field areas, the soldiers' day never ended. They lived in their uniforms, always alert, with weapons loaded and ready. Camaraderie between soldiers and disciplined benevolence of the hierarchy rendered this regimentation bearable. Ten months of this life and the journey home would seem to be a trip to paradise.

When his son was at home, the old man would wake up him up in the morning with a cup of tea and sit and listen to the stories of his son's regiment. The old man had never been a soldier. He had owned a bit of land where he had farmed for a living as had his father and grandfather before him. A well-heeled and politically connected automobile manufacturer was looking for land to establish a manufacturing unit. When the car factory was set up, they had taken over his farm. He had a small pension given by the company. But he had nothing to do.

The old man had had two sons. He was young then and a doting father. He assumed that his sons would take over the yoke of farming off him when they were older. There was a government school in the neighboring village. His wife would trek the five-mile path with her two sons in tow in the mornings. She carried with her, packed rotis for lunch. A kind Head-Master gave her the job of an attendant. The salary was a pittance, but the work kept her occupied when classes were on. School would finish by four in the evening. They would wait another hour for the sun to subside a bit before heading back.

Puttu was in class 9 when his brother died. The younger boy picked up some chest infection from school. The next morning, he was too ill to walk. He stayed back at home while Puttu and his mother made their daily pilgrimage. The fever worsened during the day. Alone at home, the boy could do nothing but cry. He became delirious and started throwing fits. When puttu and his mother got back, the boy was unconscious and quite blue.

The district hospital was a day's journey by bullock cart. By the time they took him there, he was in extremis. The doctors there had put in a half-hearted struggle to save him. But medicines were in short supply and the doctors shackled by inexperience and prejudice. the boy passed away the same night. Puttu' mother died soon thereafter, of a broken heart. Her younger son had been her favorite and after he died, she just wasted away.

Puttu was alone with his father. After his father left for the fields, Puttu would trek to school alone. A kindly teacher arranged for his daily lunch. He passed his tenth when an army recruitment team had come to their school. Any boy who was selected by them would be educated for another two years at government expense before being absorbed into the army. Puttu and his father discussed the opportunity. Being in the army was prestigious. He would be rated high in the matrimonial market. His wife and her family would be a source of support for his dad.

Farm work had stopped now. Land acquisition was in progress. Puttu's dad had little to do and lots of time. Most of his associates had moved to towns where jobs were available. Puttu was in the army and happy in his regiment. His father stayed back, making incremental improvements to their house with regular remittances from Puttu.

Today, the village had changed. The car company had transformed the area. A township had sprung up a kilometer from where the old man lived, with its own hospital and school. The little house they possessed in ten cents of land was worth a packet today. Roads, shops and movie halls were in the vicinity.

. The train station was at the town of Kanshi. From there, Puttu would have to catch a bus to his village. Their house was close to a new state highway now. An express bus from the district headquarters would be coming in an hour and his son would be on it. The old man had had an anxious year. Puttu was now posted in the mountains. The area was infested with insurgents. There was a constant danger of being ambushed or blown up. But his Puttu was safe. He had rung up the post master from the base camp yesterday to say that he was on his way.

The tea kettle was boiling. The old man put in the tea leaves and a bit of milk. He never cooked when he was alone. He had a running account with the village canteen and ate all his meals there. When Puttu came home, it was different. Father and son would share the cooking and the tea making.

It was time for the bus. The old man covered the tea pot with a cover. Giving his mustache a final twill, he picked up his lathi and set out for the bus stand. He did not really need the stick's help. It was more a question of habit. There was a time, when he was a farmer, when the stick came in handy. He used it to drive out cattle, straying into the paddy fields or to chase away the boys who would steal his mangoes. He looked around. Now the mango trees were gone and the fields had been razed. The air of the village was not the same. There was a smell of smoke and oil and the ceaseless rumble of machinery in the background.

There was an old banyan tree by the road side, where the bus would stop. The tree was older than the man. Indeed, it had been fully grown when he was still a child. He could see the bus in the distance now. The mud tracks had been replaced by a long straight concrete road. There was an unending stream of trucks and car containers looking like so many ants crawling down the stark landscape. The distinctive red and yellow of the bus could be made out at the horizon.

The car company had been generous to the farmers. A colony had been made for the villagers at the district head-quarters. Employment preference was given to suitable denizens of the locality. Most of the villagers had moved to the colony. Property prices were higher her. There were schools and colleges and hospitals. The company provided a free bus servic e for workers from the colony to the factory premises.

Some of the displaced farmers sold their new houses for a princely amount and had moved elsewhere. He peered down the highway. It would take the bus another thirty minutes to reach. The old man squatted under a tree and waited.

He had a surprise for Puttu. He had found the girl who would be Puttu's wife. She was the daughter of a neighboring village Pramukh. The girl was pretty and the Pramukh a man of substance. After all, Puttu was a handsome man. He was a soldier in the Indian Army. He could definitely become a Subedar one day. The old man's heart was overflowing with pride.

The bus came to a halt. A young man had disembarked. Where was Puttu? The conductor was pointing towards the old man. The bus moved on. The old man watched with a strange foreboding as the young stranger walked towards him. "Are you Puttu's father?", the young man was asking. The old man nodded in the affirmative. "I am Raj. I am from Puttu's unit. We were traveling together. Last evening some intoxicated college students had got into the train. They carried guns and knives. They were drinking and creating a nuisance. No one had dared to interfere. When they started molesting one of the lady passengers, Puttu jumped to the rescue. One of the men had shot him in the head. They had then jumped off the train and escaped. By the time, the train came to a stop at the next station, Puttu was dead".

The old man swayed, holding on to his stick. Raj was supporting him now., as he walked over to the tree and sat down, head in his hands. Puttu was dead. Raj was still talking. He would go with the old man to the town to collect Puttu's body after the postmortem. The unit would be sending more people to organize the final rites. For the old man, nothing registered. The sun was high up in the sky and there was little shade under the tree. But he refused to move. He, like the tree, had nowhere to go.

****

The Woman

She looked at the man sleeping on the bed. He was big built and hairy and snored a bit. He seemed quite oblivious to being watched. It was getting late now.  The clock had chimed four and the milkman would be knocking at the door by five. If he saw the man in her house, her reputation would be ruined.

There was a time, when she would have decided to dare it. "To hell with what people thought". She had been younger then. Now she was possibly wiser. "If she were wise – why would she land up with this hairy stranger 'snoring on her bed?'. Susan had no answer to that.

It was almost three years since she had done anything remotely as crazy. Three years since Raj had left for his job in Dubai, with promises to write daily. She had received a dozen letters in the first month, but then they had stopped. Two months after he left, Susan heard from a friend that Raj was dating a nurse in the Government Hospital. Susan had been bitter at first. But life had to move on.

Her office friends had been very supportive. They had even tried to play cupid and to introduce her to eligible and willing young men. Susan had thought she was past it. She and Raj had a passionate affair which lasted over three years. They had met at office, when both of them joined the Marine Products Company. It was love at first sight or so it seemed. "To Raj – it must just have been lust" – thought Susan with a twinge of remorse.

She had taken good care of him. They had hired adjacent flats – but lived together. Susan used to comment that Raj's bed had never been slept in.

She looked at the sleeping giant again. He was stirring now. The light was disturbing him – but he seemed to be a slow waker. Raj had been different; he had been slim and lithe and used to wake up before her. He would make coffee for them both and then go across to his flat – where he would sit at his computer for an hour – before going to office.

The man had opened his eyes now. She desperately, tried to remember his name. It was Ram something. How could you call a man Ram - after sleeping shamelessly with him.

It had been totally unplanned. He had stood uncomfortably close to her in the crowded bus. Her friends had gone their separate ways from the movie hall, with their spouses and girl-friends. Cathy and her friend Tom could have dropped her back at her place as they usually did and all this would not have happened. But Cathy had been feeling a little unwell and maybe she had resented Tom's interest in Susan. Tom was plain stupid. He had kept touching her and cozying up all through the movie. How could he be stupid enough to think that Cathy would not realize what was going on.

Susan had been glad, when the bus left, leaving Cathy with her frosty stares behind. She had been too engrossed in thought to notice the man who had insinuated himself close to her. When she looked at him sternly, he looked away. Susan was in no mood to create a scene. When he had followed her out of the bus and asked her obviously irrelevant directions, she should have walked away. He had talked her into offering him coffee at her place. "The rest" – she thought, was history.

He was sitting up in bed now. Susan passed him a mug of coffee, which he accepted without a smile or a "thank you". She left the room as he dressed.

She would ring up Cathy and apologize for Tom's behavior later. The bedroom door opened and the man emerged. He was all charm again, but they were both in a hurry to say good bye.

Closing the door, she returned to the bed room to tidy up. Five minutes later the bell rang. It was the milk man. She set about making some breakfast. She would call Cathy at 6 AM.

It was six now. She opened her purse for her phone. She was shocked to find that her i-phone which was her 27th birthday's self-gift was missing. Gone also was her money and credit cards.

Susan sat at the edge of the bed and sobbed.

*****

The Space Machine

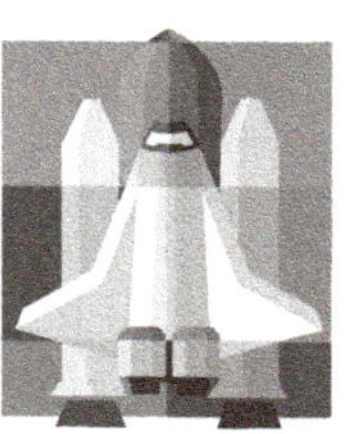

Rekha Singh was a talented girl. Her parents were busy doctors at the Government Hospital. Rekha was their only child. She was a good student. Bright and likeable, her friends and teachers assumed that she would one day follow her parent's footsteps. But Rekha had a mind of her own.

She was fascinated by astronomy and mathematics. She surprised everyone by opting for the engineering stream. Her parents were a little concerned. They felt ill equipped to guide their daughter through a field that was alien to them. However, Rekha's resolve was firm and her persistence won the day.

Selection to the Institutes of Technology was tough. Rekha was pleasantly surprised when the results of the IIT entrance examination was declared. She was in the first ten of the merit list and could get the subject of her choice, in the institute of her choice. She chose aerospace engineering. The rest was history.

The field of aerospace engineering had literally exploded over the next few years. Reusable rocket technology made space travel affordable. The development of a photon engine by the Kuwamoto team was poised to revolutionize space exploration. These machines could tap into the recently discovered photon belts. Photon belts or beams were the energy bands that literally held the universe together.

With the capacity to detect and enter a photon beam, one could travel around these bands at the speed of light without encountering any of the mass augmentations predicted by earlier physicists. Another development which provided a magnum jump in our space capability was the development of the atomic synthesizer. By agitating atoms of any material within the synthesizer they were broken down to sub nuclear particles. By using a version of an atomic sieve one could ensure that only the random combinations we desired exited the machine. It was a futuristic alchemy machine. As mans greed for gold had abated, the machines were designed to create carbon and oxygen atoms. This would provide endless food and oxygen for space travel. The sky was no longer the limit.

Rekha was a brilliant student. Indian girls had etched their names in the archives of space travel. NASA was on the lookout for talented and dedicated young minds to induct into their space travel program. There were risks involved and her parents were worried. But Rekha's dogged determination won the day. Within a month of her graduation from the IIT she was in a giant space training module run by NASA. She along with the two other girls, one from Texas and another from France were preparing for what was described as the voyage of the century. There would be photon thrust machines with the carbon oxygen synthesizers-each manned by a single girl.

With the thrust vectoring of the photon engines their machines would be traveling at the speed of light. The mass of the machine would, by conventional scientific wisdom, augment itself to infinity. Yet the beauty of the photon machine lay in the machines capacity to use this mass for providing additional thrust. The space riders had only to find proton streams, to accelerate then to the speed of light. From then on; the machine would self-support its propulsion energy need, shedding mass to perpetuate motion.

The photon core would isolate the astronauts. Photon streaming would prevent the inmates from the imponderables of the speed of light. By harnessing photons, a major bugbear had been overcome.

The great day dawned. The three space riders stepped in to their space mobiles. The common booster which would thrust them beyond the limits of earth's gravitational field was lit. Whoosh- the trio disengaged from the thruster rockets. They whizzed past the solar system planets. They were soon scanning for the photon streams which would whisk them through the galax, at many times the speed of light.

Riding or surfing photon beams was a navigational feat never achieved or attempted before. Unmanned craft had been photon beam streamed. Retrieval however had not been possible even with AI powered systems. Once in a photon stream you were not contactable by any signal. AI did not have enough power of the will to navigate itself out of the belt. You needed a human with a sense of purpose. The three of them had navigated upon and exited photon streams in computer simulations. Would it work in real life when you were hurtling along at many times the speed of light.

Minerva, the most daring of the trio, was the first to detect a photon stream. I am off – she screamed. She dropped from their lidar screen and now they could see her only on their virtual interface pads. Following Minerva, Rekha and Katrina were also sucked into the photon stream.

Rekha watched in astonishment as her speed indicator- climbed straight to 'C' this indicated that the space craft was now traveling at the speed of light. There was no apparent increase in the size of her machine. The scientists at the giant simulator complex were right. As long as she stayed on in the photon stream- there would be no mass changes. "When in Rome- do as the Romans do" Rekha laughed to herself. She was traveling in a beam of light. Here the speed of light was the norm. The galactic observation cameras were doing their jobs.

Photo memories were being recorded. These records which would take the largest quantum computers back home months to evaluate were being encrypted by the nano second. Photon belts held the universe together. Galaxies streaming away from the big bang were constrained within the limits of the photon belts.

Stellar systems would bounce off the photon restraints. reversal of trajectories was earlier recorded as negative energy and the transition phase recorded as black holes. Black holes and negative energy were a hazard for space voyagers. If you were sucked into one you would emerge in another dimension. What this dimension was yet to be deciphered by science. Rekha was glad she was in the confines of the photon belt. Here, you were protected and insulated from black hole and myriad occult vagaries of the universe.

This was truly the ultimate in free rides. Photon beams had elliptical courses. In a decade or two the particular beam would drop them back near the solar system again. It was postulated that a time warp would restore them to contemporary time slots. Rekha and her co astronauts were aware that the time warp might not work. The concept of light and of Time being bent was still based on mathematical gymnastics. Would it work in real time? If the time warp did not follow light warping they would be stuck. In that case it was possible that they would land on earth a few decades later. They would not have aged within the Proton Beam. Their friends would be in late middle age.

Where the photon belt returned near our galaxy the girls would need to execute a series of acrobatic navigational loops. Their galactic navigation systems would give them plenty of notice, weeks in advance, when they could maneuver their crafts to the beams periphery. Here the girls would start a deceleration process which would permit them to escape within the range of the solar system and home. During their sojourn in space millions of signals would be sent out and received. If there were intelligent creatures out there- they would know that the girls had come calling.

As Rekha glanced at the speed indicator she received a jolt. The needle had moved well beyond 'C' and was touching 'C2' which meant that she was traveling of twice the speed of light. This was a concept that was not fully accepted. But she was now proving it. The speed of the light was not constant after all. The core of the proton beam was faster than what anyone had predicted. The speedometer

had jammed now. But the electric indicator kept blinking. C4-C10-C100- she must have reached the core of the beam by now.

The space mobiles were cruising at hundred times the speed of light. The cameras were clicking. The girls studied the images with wonder. In the Galaxy of Stargeon they saw a million space ships. They saw giant cities in space with creatures of all descriptions. Flying together in formation- well outside the photon beam they did not notice the space girls. There was no scope of interaction. By the time the camera recorded the images they were a hundred light years away. There would be no social calls.

The alarm in the space craft went off. Their Galactic Positioning system suggested possible exits near the solar system in a light year. The girls went into frenetic activity. At 100° C speeds they would have to get out of the beam in 3 days.

Rockets were started and boosters used. As they moved away from the core of the beam- there was turbulence. But the girls were well trained.

They were out of the Photon beam now. Rockets still desperately slowing them down from their sling shot speeds as they are entered the solar system. The familiar sight of the rings of Saturn seemed strangely nostalgic.

A journey which would have taken then a decade had been completed in a week. Could it be that they have gained this time. The phenomenon of the time warp could consider while traveling faster than sound. By earthly laws the speed of light was still considered absolute. They were descending through the earth's atmosphere now. Thermal protection screens glowed a dull red as they descended- their fall slowly by great parachutes. The Cape Carnevel Air strip was on the radar. They prepared their engines for a powered landing. Voices could be heard as Rekha slowed down for a touch-down. "Slow down, slow down" the voice sounded familiar.

She felt a tap on her shoulder. Her father was sitting behind her in the car. How many times I told not you, not to day dream while you are driving. There were other vehicles on the road. Familiar sights of the MG Road and the Marz o Rin brought her back to the present. Was it a dream, or had she come back to the past. There was no way Rekha could find all.

That evening at dinner, they sat and debated over Rekha's future plans. She should have to decide her choices of subjects for the eleventh class. "Are you still adamant on your aerospace engineering". "Yes" said Rekha. The future was strange and exciting.

*****

The Astrologer

It was a busy day in the out-patient clinic. There were irate women, with kids in tow. Families with a free day had decided to check out all their minor ailments. There were young men in search of a day's medical leave. Older man wanted their blood pressures checked. Even Mona Lisa could not have smiled through all this. I was trying my best.

Queue jumpers are the bane of busy outpatient clinics in government hospitals. One had to attend to the serious patients out of turn. This was acceptable. Anther irritant was a patient proclaiming his or her own importance. Patients who seemed more intent on establishing their credentials were asking for trouble. The middle aged Sardarji who was seated opposite me now, was doing exactly that. He showed me his personnel file. There were letters of appreciation from luminaries in various fields. I surmised that the man was an astrologer. Politely pushing aside, the indexed newspaper cuttings I cut short the introductions. Could I help him?

He was a little hurt. I did not have to be an astrologer to see that. I ordered a sonogram to evaluate the cause of his enlarged liver. There was an abscess in the liver. It was probably due to amoebiasis. I referred him to the appropriate specialist. The gentle man however insisted on having the last word. "You will settle abroad" he told me. He wished me all the best and left.

Years passed. I went through specialization and sub specialization. I remembered the old man's prediction. It seemed less likely by the day. I was well settled in my job. It was not easy for neurosurgeons to migrate abroad. There were credentialing procedures which were quite cumbersome. My only visit outside the country had been to Bangladesh. The old man had missed, by a mile.

I was pushing fifty when fate churned up my career. Suddenly life did not seem as predictable as it had been, before. There were twists and turns. The job offer from Toronto was a welcome surprise.

I met him at the Mumbai air-port. With my presbyopia and preoccupations, I did not recognize the old Sardarji who shuffled towards me till we spoke. You must come back home, often, he cautioned me. My memory haze cleared. I recognized the old astrologer now.

At the Toronto hospital the director was giving me options. I could hire a two-room run up or invest in the ownership of a flat. As my contract was a short one, rental might be more appropriate. I opted for ownership. I had started believing my astrologer.

****

The Healer from Hazratganj

Bazeed Khan was a successful businessman. He inherited a defunct grocery store from an heirless uncle. It would be an uphill task to try and restart a business in rural Maharashtra. Bribes would have to be paid. Extortions from local politicians and criminal elements was inevitable. Bazeed, refused to be stared down by odds. With honest wholesome grit, sagely patience and diligent hard work he built up a popular mini bazaar. Khan's supermarket sold everything from tomatoes to television sets. He walked the extra mile to make sure that his clients got the best possible deals. Forgoing easy pickings, he forged a formidable reputation for reliability.

Bazeed's wife, Salma was educated. She had completed her graduation from the Wilson College, at Bombay, with distinction. Turning down a spate of good job offers; she opted to be a house wife and a homemaker. Bazeed was a good husband. He and Salma were blessed with a baby daughter within a year of their marriage. They named the baby Jemima.

All seemed well with Jemima till she was three months old. Then one day, after a short crying spell- Jemima started turning blue. Bazeed and Salma had rushed down, with their baby, to a multi-specialty hospital, which was just a couple of blocks down the road. Financed by a Japanese conglomerate, the hospital was optimally equipped and efficiently run.

There was no time wasted. A team of competent doctors had resuscitated her. A cardiology team was called in to perform what they called a Balloon Septostomy. The crisis was successfully tackled. After the procedure, doctors counseled the worried parents. Definitive corrective surgery would be needed. The sooner it was done, the better. Waiting too long would result in Pulmonary artery hypertension. This would compromise long term outcomes. Treatment would be expensive. Pediatric Cardiac surgery in the private sector could cost a packet.

Bazeed had invested well. A prudently taken insurance policy ensured that the family could afford Jemima's treatment. Financial issues aside, there were daunting technical challenges. The cardiac surgery team had a planning session. After a detailed evaluation of images, they called Jemima's parents. They were concerned that an anomalous blood vessel which was visualized during Jemima's pre-operative workup could pose problems during surgery. There were no other options. Bazeed requested them to go ahead.

Jemima was wheeled into the OR at 7 in the morning. Bazeed and Salma waited anxiously. It was well past lunchtime when the chief surgeon came out. The surgeon's concerns were right. Every attempt to reposition the arteries was met with bizarre and hazardous rhythm disturbances. After a marathon session lasting eight hours, they abandoned the procedure. Jemima was alive- but her heart anomaly persisted. The consensus was that the electrical syncytium of the myocardium was too immature. A second attempt would be made when Jemima was a year old.

The surgical team, which would attempt Jemimas re-do surgery, prepared with diligence. Expert opinions were sought from the best centers in the world, in Paris and London. Without surgical correction it was unlikely that Jemima would live long enough to attend school. Five days after she completed a year of age, Jemima was operated upon. This time around, every contingency had been catered for, every step rehearsed- but at the end of twelve hours the surgeons gave up. The surgical verdict was final. Jemima's cardiac defect could not be repaired. To carry on with surgery could be fatal. With the defect she could pull on for another three to four years at most.

After the failure of the second surgery, Bazeed and Salma reconciled themselves to what seemed inevitable. They showered Jemima with love and affection. They ensured that she attended pre-school with the other children. They also decided against any further expansion of the family.

When Jemima was three years old, Bazeed had a visitor. An elderly hakim, related to Salma, dropped in. He brought with him Mehboob. Bazeed remembered Mehboob. The man had been a vegetable vendor with an iconic hand cart well known to the women in the township. Unfortunately, Mehbbob had fallen very ill. The last Bazeed heard of him was that Mehboob was on his deathbed in a hospice.

The hakim told Bazeed of the healer from Hazratgang. 'Bakim Baba'. as the healer was popularly called, ran a practice that did not conform to any known system of medicine. Yet he had acquired a mystical skill and a massive reputation of curing the most complex illnesses-considered incurable by competent specialist teams. Bazeed was a rational and pragmatic man. He gave no credence to what were bizarre and tall claims. The story recounted by Mehboob-the vegetable vendor, in person, dissipated his cynicism.

Mehboob had been diagnosed by the doctors of the regional cancer hospital to have a cancer of his liver. The disease had spread and the doctors had declared the condition inoperable. It was at this juncture that Mehboob had heard of the Baba. Though the Baba gave no guarantees, he charged no fees either. Mehboob had no money and no other options. He attended the Baba's clinic at the outskirts of Paswan village. The Baba listened patiently while Mehboob recited his medical history. He then wrapped a Muslin cloth around Mehboob's mid-section, before sending him off for the night. Mehboob slept in a make shift communal shelter, which was surprisingly well maintained. In the morning the Baba examined

Mehmood. The muslin cloth was unraveled. On the cloth there was a writing, which Mehboob swore-was not there before. The Baba read it and proclaimed that the surgery would be performed the same night.

That night Mehboob was on the Baba's operation couch, in front of an audience of the devout. A shiny dagger glistened in the Baba's hand, which he plunged towards Mehboob's abdomen. Mehboob winced- anticipating pain- but he felt nothing. The Baba now thrust his hand into Mehmood's abdomen. Minutes later, the hand emerged, holding in it an evil looking lump of tissues. A salve followed by a sliver of muslin made up the wound dressing. The next morning, one of Baba's assistants ripped off the muslin. There had been no scar to show for the night's dramatics. A month later, when Mehboob visited the cancer center, the doctors were amazed. The tumor seemed to have receded dramatically.

Bazeed, against his better judgement was intrigued. It was obvious that Jemima was running out of time. Her blue spells had become more frequent. There was a glazed look in her eyes all the time. Jemima was wilting. Bazeed talked it over with Salma. They pondered over the possibilities for almost a month before accepting the obvious. There were no options. Logic succumbed to emotions. After tying up a few odds, and ends, they drove down to the Baba's farm.

The Baba conducted his clinic in a long shed shaded by fruit trees. Children played in the surrounding fields. Luxury cars parked in the shade attested to the opulence of at least some of the hundred odd visitors. The Bazeed family joined in the long queue that would bring them to the Baba's presence. There were stretchers with patients of varying ages and ailments. Then there were mothers like Salma carrying their ailing children. Each patient would be stopped in front of the Baba who would place his hand on their foreheads before muttering something incomprehensible. The Baba's assistants would then do the dispensing. It was the occasional patient that the Baba chose for surgery. Ten of these chosen had been told to come again, at night for their procedures. Jemima was one of them.

That night Bazeed and Salma, along with Jemima were seated in front of the podium where the Baba performed his miracle surgeries. What happened in the next few hours would have appeared gruesome and macabre in any context. However, the air was so surcharged with expectancy and faith that no one recoiled or fainted.

Five patients and their relatives found a semicircle around the Dias. The Baba entered, dressed in Jeans and a T shirt. He was followed by two assistants in white robes who were swaying rhythmically in a drugged or spiritual stupor. There was a stone bed in the center of the Dias partially covered by a green baize cloth. An earthen tray propped up by a wooden trident contained a bunch of gruesome looking instruments.

A lady with an incurable cancer of her ovary was carried to the dais and laid on the stone table. Her cheeks were pinched and there was no flesh on her bones. Yet her eyes were shining with the light of hope. Her body seemed to be wracked by periodic spasms of agony. The healer moved over to the lady. His walk and demeanor had changed. He spoke in a guttural voice in a language that sounded like Russian, as if to someone in the room, the others could not perceive. Raising a knife in the air, he plunged it into the lady's abdomen. As the onlookers watched, enthralled, he inserted his hand into the gaping wound [which- mysteriously did not bleed]. The hand emerged- with a mass of bloody flesh, which the Baba held out for all to see- rather like a conjuror bringing out a rabbit from a hat. An assistant passed a salve and a bandage to the Baba, which he used, to seal off the wound. The Baba drenched in sweet was helped back into a side room. The first operation was over.

Then, it was Jemima's turn. Her eyes were full of peace, seeming not to share the anxiety of her parents. She was laid down on the stone table. The Baba reentered the arena. His mannerisms seemed strangely effeminate. He spoke now with musical lilt. Salma who had taken French in school found some words strongly familiar. The healer raised his arm and Bazeed closed his eyes.

He opened his eyes to find the healer holding something in his hand, which was pounding and pulsating in obvious chaos. Bazeed gasped when he realized that the healer was holding Jemima's deformed heart. As the healer kneaded the heart in to shape, applying a salve, the rhythm of pulsation seemed to settle. It was a while before the heart was pushed back into the child's chest. A salve and bandage followed. Jemima was handed back to her parents. She opened her eyes at Salma's touch, smiled and went off to sleep again.

The next morning, one of Baba's assistants removed her bandage. Jemima and her parents returned to the Baba's office, but were turned away. The job had been done and the Baba wanted no payment. A sealed envelope was given to Bazeed, to be opened on Jemima's 25th birthday.

When Jemima was taken back for a cardiology review the doctor mumbled something about spontaneous correction. Bazeed never took her back to the hospital again except for her immunization shots and later for braces to set her shiny teeth.

Jemima was cured. A week after surgery, she was playing games and outrunning a few boys. She grew up as a vivacious young girl. She was brilliant in academics and had only vague distorted memories of an Auntie Jeanne who had operated upon her at Lourdes. There were so many imponderables in the whole affair that Bazeed and Salma did not bother to correct her.

Jemima joined medical school and was an excellent student. She had a fondness for little children and for cardiology. She finished her medical school crowned with awards and immersed in honors. Her selection on a European fellowship to her choice of institutes surprised no one. The hospital for sick children in Paris was the best in the world. Jemima joined the hospital for apprenticeship in Paediatric cardiology. Her parents shrugged off pressures from the orthodox to marry her off to a suitable Muslim boy. Jemima had character and conviction. She was surely entitled to a freedom of choice.

It was towards the third year of her Pediatric cardiology apprenticeship that Jemima met Pierre. Pierre was a brilliant Pediatric heart surgeon at the institute. His mother, Maire-Jeanne Lappier had established one of the finest departments in the world. Her unexpected tragic death in a car accident more than 20 years ago had deprived the world of one of its finest surgeons. Many doctors in France felt that Pierre was the one surgeon who could restore the department to its former glory.

Although he was considered to be one of the most eligible bachelors in Paris, Pierre lead an austere life. He was attracted to Jemima by her innocence and the burning intensity of her professional commitment which matched his own. They worked together and they fell in love.

Pierre and Jemima were married in a quaint French cathedral. Her parents and a few friends from India attended the ceremony along with a sizeable gathering of the cream of Paris society. Pierre knew that Jemima had undergone some corrective cardiac surgery in her childhood.

Jemima one day confided in him of the story her parents had told her about a faith healer who had cured her disease.

Over coffee and a cucumber sandwich in the hospital canteen Jemima relived her memories of childhood with Pierre. Jemima's memory of her final operation was an enigma. She vaguely remembered a hospital named Lourdes and a lovely lady who operated upon her. Jemima recollected her surgeon's name as Auntie Jeanne. She surmised that these were just figments of a child's imagination. She looked up at Pierre whose face was aglow with the lumiscent radiance of love and discovery. Pierre was sure now that Jemima was not confabulating. Jemima's memories and narrative were stridently and spectacularly clear.

Pierre's emotions were whirling. There were too many truths and improbable co-incidences. He held his head in his hands. Jemima sensed Pierres consternation and went over to him. It took Pierre a while to clear his head. Pierre motioned to Jemima to sit down. His voice brimmed over with emotion as he spoke. The children's hospital of Paris had been popularly known as Lourdes many years ago. Pierre's mothers name was Jeanne. He hurried to his locker and took out a photograph. He brought it over for Jemima to see. Jemima was stunned- 'that is Auntie Jeanne-she said'. "No!" corrected Pierre," That was my mother."

Pierre recounted the day she died on the 4th August of 1967. Madam Jeanne had left home early that morning. For the past few days, she had been immersed in her operative atlas as she prepared to perform a complex Pediatrics Cardiac corrective surgery. The fog which submerged Paris was unusually dense. Streetlights were dull glows by the roadside. The roads were empty and slithery with fog and oil. Madam Jeanne was in a hurry. She drove fast, with her characteristic surgeon's impatience. Her car had veered off the bridge, that misty Paris morning.

A search was launched for her later in the day when she did not turn up at the hospital. The police fished her car out of the river, but her body had never been found. There was one mystery which had never been explained. The hospital records had not shown any surgery scheduled for the day.

Jemima remembered the old brown envelope which her father had given her. She and Pierre searched for it. Together they retrieved it from Jemima's locker. The outer cover was a dirty brown, smudged with age and moss. They tore it open. Inside was an envelope containing a detailed description of a complex cardiac anomaly. It was signed by Marie Jeanne La Pierre- Pierre's mom, and it was dated 04 Aug 1967. Prof. Pierre had kept her surgical appointment.

****

www.ingramcontent.com/pod-product-compliance
Lightning Source LLC
Chambersburg PA
CBHW040111150726
48005CB00013B/1656